The Wishing Fish

By Jean Warren

Illustrated by Barb Tourtillotte

Warren Publishing House, Inc., P.O. Box 2250, Everett, WA, 98203, 1-800-334-4769.

Printed in Hong Kong by Mandarin Offset.
First Edition   10 9 8 7 6 5 4 3 2 1

Library of Congress Cataloging in Publication Information

Warren, Jean, 1940-
        The wishing fish / by Jean Warren ; illustrated by Barb Tourtillotte. — 1st ed.
            p.   cm.
        Summary: with the help of two magical fish, an evergreen tree and a palm tree exchange habitats but soon learn to be thankful for what they had in the first place. Includes related songs, handicraft activities, and recipes.

        ISBN 0-911019-74-X : $5.95

        [1. Trees—Fiction. 2. Wishes—Fiction. 3. Magic—Fiction. 4. Stories in rhyme.]
I. Tourtillotte, Barb, 1955- ill. II. Title.
PZ8.3.W2459Wi 1993
[E]—dc20   93-12523
                                                                 CIP
                                                                 AC

Warren Publishing House, Inc. would like to acknowledge the following activity contributors:

Barbara B. Fleisher, Glen Oaks, NY
Judith McNitt, Adrian, WI
Kay Roozen, Des Moines, IA
Sherry Sanchez, Phoenix, AZ
Betty Silkunas, Lansdale, PA

The Wishing Fish

Warren Publishing House, Inc.

Way up north
Lived a little fir tree,
Who stood in the snow
By the big North Sea.

The fir tree thought
The snow was fun,
But he often wished
He lived in the sun.

Way down south
Lived a little palm tree,
Who stood in the sun
By the big South Sea.

She loved the sun,
But do you know?
She wished she lived
Where it would snow.

Now out in the sea
Lived two special fish,
Who had the power
To grant you a wish.

"I want to go south,"
The fir did sigh,
Just as one fish
Came swimming by.

"I want to go north!"
Cried the little palm tree,
As the other fish
Swam by in the sea.

The trees got their wish
On that very same day.
They both went to lands
Far, far away.

The fir tree loved
The sun in the sky,
But soon his branches
Began to dry.

The palm tree loved
To watch the snow,
But soon her branches
Were too cold to grow.

"Oh, dear me,"
Both trees did cry.
"If we stay much longer,
We surely will die!

"We should have been happy,
We should have been glad,
With where we lived,
With what we had!"

The trees had a problem,
And that was no lie.
Lucky for them,
The fish swam back by.

"We wish," cried the trees,
"No more to roam!
If only we could
Go back to our home."

Presto! Like magic,
Their wishes came true.
Both trees were back home
With branches all new.

And, never again
Did they wish to be
Anywhere else,
But by their own sea.

Storytime Fun

Snowflakes Falling

Sung to: "Mary Had a Little Lamb"

Snowflakes falling

From the sky,

From the sky,

From the sky.

Snowflakes falling

From the sky

To the earth below.

Watch them as they

Dance and whirl,

Dance and whirl,

Dance and whirl.

Watch them as they

Dance and whirl,

Soft white winter snow.

Judith McNitt

Sing a Song of Winter

Sung to: "Sing a Song of Sixpence"

Sing a song of winter,

Frost is in the air.

Sing a song of winter,

Snowflakes everywhere.

Sing a song of winter,

Hear the sleigh bells chime.

Can you think of anything

As nice as winter time?

Judith McNitt

Summer, Summer
Sung to: "Old MacDonald Had a Farm"

Summer, summer is such fun,

Yes, oh, yes, it is.

There's so much that you can do,

Yes, oh, yes, there is.

You can go to the pool and

  keep real cool,

Jump right in and take a swim.

Summer, summer is such fun,

Yes, oh, yes, it is.

Summer, summer is such fun,

Yes, oh, yes, it is.

There's so much that you can do,

Yes, oh, yes, there is.

You can get a tan or sit on the sand,

Swim in the sea or play catch with me.

Summer, summer is such fun,

Yes, oh, yes, it is.

Barbara B. Fleisher

Sing a Song of Sunshine
Sung to: "Sing a Song of Sixpence"

Sing a song of sunshine,

Be happy every day.

Sing a song of sunshine,

You'll chase the clouds away.

Be happy every moment,

No matter what you do.

Just sing and sing and sing and sing,

And let the sun shine through!

Jean Warren

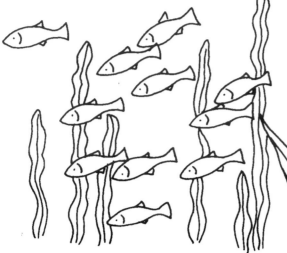

Two Rainbow Fish
Sung to: "Three Blind Mice"

Two rainbow fish,

Two rainbow fish.

See how they swim,

See how they swim?

Their tails go left and

  their tails go right,

Their beautiful colors

  are quite a sight,

Did you ever see such a sight

  so bright

As two rainbow fish?

Jean Warren

I'm a Little Fishy
Sung to: "I'm a Little Teapot"

I'm a little fishy, I can swim.

Here is my tail, here is my fin.

When I want to have fun with my

  friends,

I wiggle my tail and dive right in.

Lynn Beaird

Make a Wish

Sung to: "This Old Man"

A wishing fish came swimming by

Raised her head and winked her eye.

"Where, oh where would you like

   to be today?

Somewhere special or far away?"

"Wishing fish, wishing fish,

Would you like to know my wish?

I wish to go to _____ today,

Will you help me on my way?"

"Close your eyes, count to three,

And your wish is where you'll be."

Then the wishing fish went

Swish, swish, swish,

And at last I got my wish.

Fill in the blank line with the name of a place where you would like to be.

Jean Warren

For More Fun

• Have fun singing the story "The Wishing Fish" to the tune "On Top of Old Smokey."

• Act out the story with your friends. One person can sing the part of the palm tree, another person can sing the part of the fir tree, and two people can act out the parts of the wishing fish.

Coffee-Filter Snowflake

Decorate your room with snowflakes that won't melt!

1. Fold a coffee filter in half and then in half again.

2. Cut small triangles out of the folded edges.

3. Unfold the filter to see the snowflake you have created.

For More Fun

• Cut different shapes, such as half circles or squares, out of the folded edges.

• Use an eyedropper to drop paint onto your coffee filter before you cut it into a snowflake.

You Will Need
a coffee filter • scissors

Sun Puppet

1-2.   3-4.

Brighten your day with a Sun Puppet!

1. Cut two small circles out of yellow construction paper.

2. Cut yellow yarn into short pieces.

You Will Need

yellow construction paper • scissors • yellow yarn • glue • a craft stick

3. Glue the yarn pieces around the edges of one of the circles to make sun rays.

4. Glue the circles together with a craft stick handle in between.

For More Fun

• Use a felt-tip marker to draw a face on your Sun Puppet.

• Make more than one Sun Puppet and use them when you sing the summer songs on page 21.

Wave Machine

1-2.   3.   4-5.

Watch your friends rave about these waves!

1. Fill a small plastic or glass jar a little more than half full of water.

2. Add two or three drops of blue food coloring to the water and mix well.

3. Fill the rest of the jar with mineral oil. (Air bubbles could form if you don't fill the bottle all the way to the top.)

4. Put the lid on tight.

5. Hold the bottle sideways and gently tip it to create "waves."

For More Fun

• Before you add the oil and water, drop some sand and small shells into the bottle.

• Add some sequins to the water before you put in the oil.

You Will Need

small plastic or glass jar with a screw-on lid • water • blue food coloring • mineral oil

---

Fish in the Bottle

Watch these funny fish frolic!

1. Fill a clear-plastic 2-liter bottle half full of water.

2. Add a few drops of blue food coloring to the water and mix well.

3. Blow up two balloons, making them small enough to fit through the opening in the bottle.

4. Push the balloons into the bottle.

5. Make sure the rim of the bottle is dry. Then put glue around the rim of the bottle and screw the cap on tightly.

6. Hold the bottle on its side and gently rock it back and forth to make the balloon "fish" swim.

You Will Need
a clear-plastic 2-liter bottle • water • blue food coloring • two small balloons • glue

For More Fun
• Use a permanent marker to draw fins, gills, and so on, on the balloons before you blow them up.

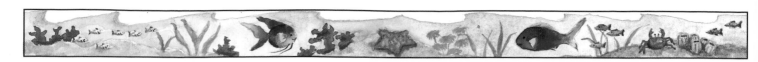

Eggshell Nursery

1-3.   **4-5.**   **6.**

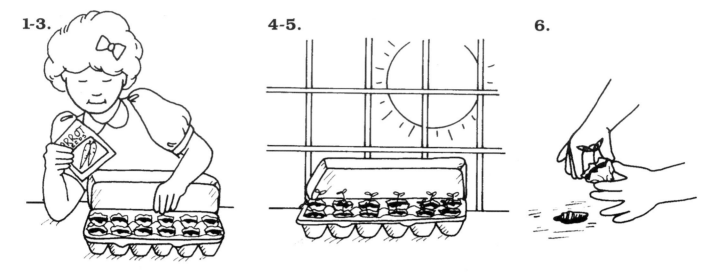

Have fun with this egg-citing garden!

1. Place empty eggshell halves in the cups of an egg carton.

2. Fill the shells with potting soil.

3. Plant one or two carrot seeds in each shell and add one tablespoon of water to each shell.

4. Close the egg carton so that the seeds will stay warm and sprout more quickly.

5. When the seeds have sprouted, open the egg-carton and set it in a warm area.

6. After the seeds have grown into seedlings, plant the eggshells outside, crushing them a little before placing them in the ground.

For More Fun

• Plant some of the seedlings in sunny areas and some in shaded areas. Watch the seedlings for a few days. Are the seedlings planted in shaded places growing as quickly as the seedlings planted in sunny areas?

You Will Need

clean eggshell halves • egg carton • potting soil • radish or carrot seeds • water

Hot and Cold Treats

Warm up or cool down with these yummy treats!

Hot Apple Cider

1. Pour apple juice into a pan.

2. Heat the juice on the stove.

3. Add a little orange juice or cranberry juice.

4. Place a cinnamon stick in the pan and simmer the cider for about 5 minutes.

5. Cool the cider until warm and serve.

You Will Need

apple juice • orange juice or cranberry juice • a cinnamon stick

Adult supervision or assistance may be required.

Grape Slush

1. Use a blender to mix the grape juice, orange-juice concentrate, water, and lemon juice together.

2. While the blender is running, drop in ice cubes, one at a time, until the mixture is slushy.

3. Pour the Grape Slush into glasses and enjoy your cool treat.

You Will Need

3 cups grape juice

1 tablespoon orange-juice concentrate

1 cup water

1 teaspoon lemon juice

Ice cubes

Tuna-Seashell Salad

1. Cook shell pasta according to the package directions.

2. Drain the shells, then let them sit in cold water until they are cool.

You Will Need

3 cups small shell pasta
1 can tuna
$\frac{1}{8}$ cup chopped pickles
$\frac{1}{8}$ cup diced celery
$\frac{1}{8}$ cup chopped green onion
$\frac{1}{8}$ cup grated carrot
2 tablespoons mayonnaise
1 tablespoon mustard
$\frac{1}{2}$ cup grated cheese

Adult supervision or assistance may be required.

Mix up a seaside snack!

3. Drain the shells again and mix them with the tuna, pickles, celery, green onion, carrot, mayonnaise, and mustard.

4. Spoon the salad into bowls and top each bowl with a little grated cheese before serving.

For More Fun

• Instead of mayonnaise and mustard use ranch, thousand island, or French salad dressing on your Tuna-Seashell Salad.

• Add a little cottage cheese to your salad.

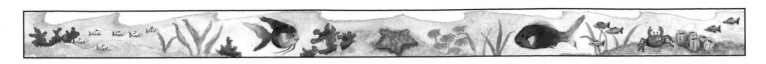

Fruit Salad Fun

Go bananas over this fruit salad!

Fruit Salad

1. Chop the apple, orange, and banana into chunks.

2. Mix all the ingredients together in a large bowl.

3. Mix in yogurt or Fruit Salad Dressing before serving.

You Will Need

1 apple
1 orange, peeled
1 banana, peeled
1 cup seedless grapes, if available
1 cup fresh or frozen berries
2 tablespoons chopped walnuts
Yogurt, any flavor, or Fruit Salad Dressing

Fruit Salad Dressing

1. Ask an adult to help you mix all the ingredients together in a blender.

2. Serve over Fruit Salad.

You Will Need

$1/4$ cup cream cheese, softened
$1/2$ banana, sliced
$1/2$ cup orange-juice concentrate

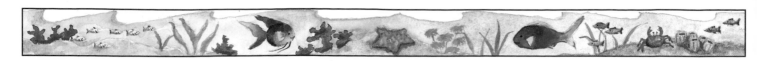

A Note to Parents and Teachers

The activities in this book have been written so that children in first, second, and third grade can follow most of the directions with minimal adult help.

The activities are also appropriate for 3- to 5-year-old children, who can easily do the suggested activities with your help.

You may also wish to extend the learning opportunities in this book by discussing climates, weather, and basic geography with your children. Point out northern and southern locations on a map. Compare dry, hot climates and damp, cool climates. Let your children decide what kinds of clothes they would pack for a trip north or south.

This is also a wonderful time to introduce or review opposites with your children. Make up word games or matching cards for opposites such as hot / cold, north / south, dry / wet, happy / sad, little / big, and so on.

Children learn so much better when they can express their ideas and feelings through age-appropriate activities. We know you'll enjoy seeing your children's eyes light up when you extend a story with related activities.